A Little Family

Short Prose Pieces

Kathryn Rantala

SPUYTEN DUYVIL
New York City

Acknowledgments:

Some of these pieces were first published by the following: *3rd Bed*, *Alice Blue Review*, *Avatar Review*, *Cake Train*, *Denver Quarterly*, *Eleven Bulls Anthology*, *The God Particle*, *elimae*, *Linnaean Street*, *Pear Noir!*, *Poems Niederngasse*, *Upstairs at Duroc*. The pieces in "The Statuary Garden" are taken from a larger memoir, *A Partial View Toward Nazareth* (Casa de Snapdragon Press, New Mexico, 2010.)

Cover illustration, *Portrait of a Girl and Her Dog* by J. Lequeu, ca. 1796,
in *The Public Domain Review*.

Illustration for "The Hunterian Museum" by Bernard Siegfried Albinus (1697-1770),
in the public domain.

For Norman Lock,

and, always, for Daris

Contents

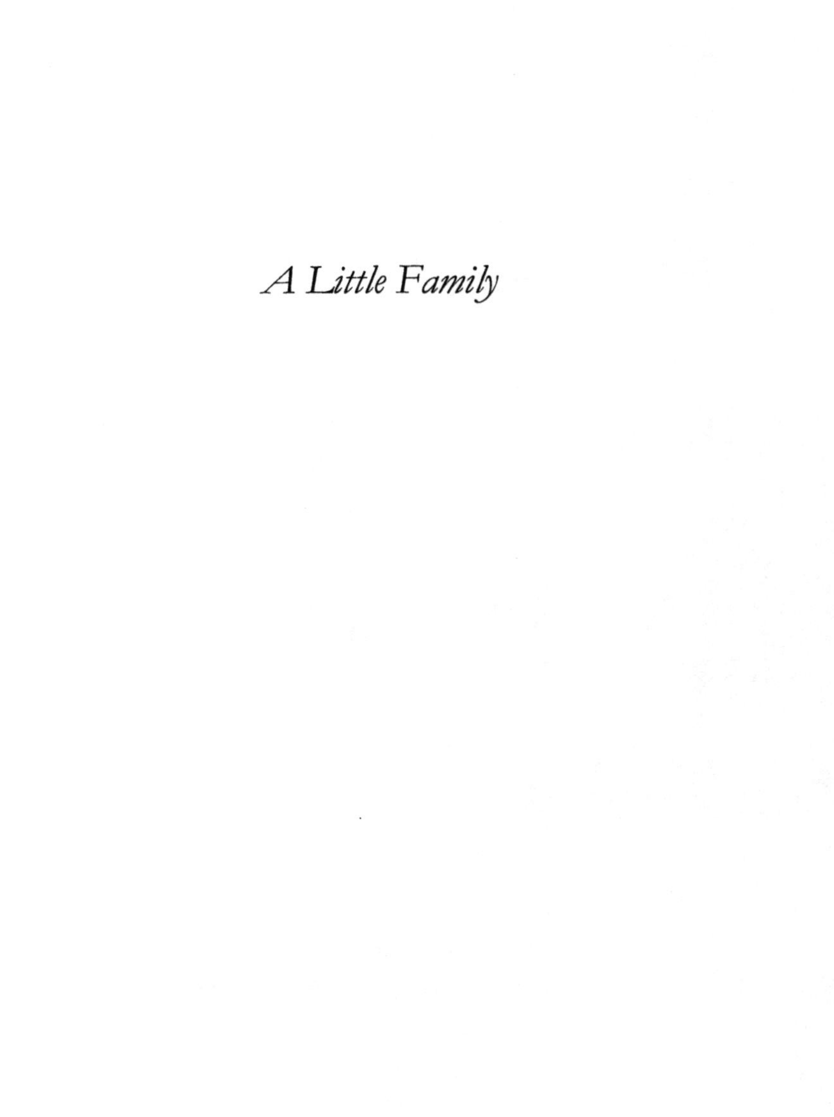

A Little Family

A Little Family

One day a little family began. It did not start out intending to be small but formed in the usual way and then, because it was attractive, gathered others to it. As the nucleus was not large or forceful, however, it did not retain its parts very well. Spouses, friends and small children flew out from time to time, as from a giant crack-the-whip, their faces lit with surprise and momentary thrill.

Charted over time, the energy of this group remained a constant, no matter its losses. The family was not unhappy; it prized itself as itself.

And little wonder. Its members captured attention like an approach of weather. Among them were—or had been— musicians, surgeons, artists, aviators, charismatics, scholars, hermits, contemplatives, woodworkers, seers, effetes, and wealthy, quixotic, generous, explosive romantics. Each flared in one or more of its interesting ways, amazing others and entertaining themselves. An Aurora Borealis of a family.

Within an aurora, streamers or arches appear, caused by the emission of light from atoms excited by electrons accelerated along magnetic lines. Similarly, families emit excitement, each according to its lights.

One day, out of the blue, perhaps from the stratosphere where weather changes but little, forces of containment began to take aim at this little family on Earth and pick off its members, one by one. The casual observer might not have noted the steadily lessening of size and influence of this already tiny group, but within it, absences were mounting like holes in the ozone.

The current hole in the ozone is now a little bigger than Antarctica.

The same observer might see the course of this family as smooth. It aged in all its levels, it got on. In close-up, however its progress was becoming as rutted as washboards, strained as cleats. Nevertheless, in trouble or at peace, it sensed its distinctions, valued its similarities, and held together whether in potato cellars or lecture circuits. An armada of a family, running seaward and generally clear of the rocks.

Armadas are made up of warships or fishing vessels or other moving gatherings of things we see, such as a belt of meteorites; also other things we do not see very well. From space our atmosphere appears as a thin blue veil sailing around the world.

The rate of meteor activity in the atmosphere is greatest near daybreak when Earth's orbital rotation is in the direction of the dawn terminator. Earth scoops up meteoroids on the morning side of the planet and outruns them on the dusk side, reminiscent of the behaviors of a following tide or a youngest child.

There is evidence in early rock formations of an anaerobic reducing atmosphere containing elements we know but in their reduced state.

The polar winter, for example, leads to the formation in the stratosphere of a vortex drawing air from the upper layers of atmosphere and lower layers of mesosphere. Stratospheric clouds comprise the home of lesser gods who, when sunlight returns to the polar regions of the hemisphere, are again able to see details of the earth faintly through holes in the ozone, the vacancies caused by chlorine and bromine compounds in catalytic destruction cycles. The gods are mildly distracted by what they can see on Earth and enhance their lazy joys by gaming. The object of one such game is to reach for what they can barely see below and remove the greatest number of them. Isolates and small groups, especially if they shine, are targets of convenience. These removals are called Chapman Reactions, in *A Theory of Upper-Atmosphere Ozone*, by S. Chapman, Member of the Royal Meteorological Society, 1930. The reactions include a sensation in mortals not unlike the sudden onset of winter.

Such a sensation may also be like a veil, of which there are many kinds: lengths of protective or ornamental netting for the head or face; any of various liturgical cloths, especially to cover a chalice; material which hides, obscures, disguises, or softens tonal distortion; interventions through which it is difficult to see; sheer things; membranes or other things covering body parts; things to be lifted or assumed by a nun.

Of all the veils, the thin blue one in particular is the most exquisite and magical.

Astoria Finns: Her Portrait

Continually added onto over the years, the original portion of the house gives way at its peak to lesser pitch. The third section, newest and less well-thought-out, if time and care may be described as thinking, leans wearily on the rest like the lid of a storm cellar; that is, prone to damage from the west. The separate shed is linked to the house by pathways, the smell of apples and dust. Astoria Finns, who lives in the house, keeps in the shed a scythe that the mice can't chew and cardboard barrels of dried corn that they can. The corn is for her chickens, though the pullets always get out and can hardly be said to be hers anymore, eating and sleeping as they do beyond the pen. She sees them from the house, nodding their greetings, pointing their slow, wrinkled feet teasingly toward the coop, clucking their descriptions of the outside world as seen from close to the ground—stories the cow is too tall to believe. Plump and generous, the hens scratch intricate maps for their chicks. Even smaller birds drop down to annotate with their tiny toes. The gracious potentials of the world cannot be exaggerated. And who could say, when the sun slips quietly down in the evening and dust devils settle and trees stop their leaves dead still, when the cow turns toward the shed and Astoria Finns turns toward the house, whether any of them think of symbiosis.

Astoria cleans up from dinner, running a cloth over stains and grooves in her table, over the complex textures of wood and wear. The next morning, as the one before it, she will go boldly in her nightclothes to the front door and throw it open on its hinges and stand where the sun can see her. The cow has rituals, too, and each night does whatever it feels like doing, bending or straightening its big knees. It faces this way or that, revisits its meals and takes something more to process. It drinks water and turns its enormous eyes toward a rat. It makes sounds and flicks its tail like a rope. If designed by its maker to dream, it does that too and in all ways behaves like its fellows. It is the cow it is, the same as those on the farms of Finland. The chickens, too, are the chickens they are.

One morning, Astoria is writing letters at her table, delaying breakfast and listening to Viennese piano music. Peace has put all its continuities on display. But when she stands to look out the window, she sees that the gate is unlatched! New chaff and small branches lean messily against the shed, leaves litter the walk, and potholes in the drive brim dangerously with water! And in the place where the god of constancy should be, clouds have lined up in front of other clouds, their blurry hands filled with portent and interruption. And in that moment of alarm the cat asks, in its way, to be let outside.

Astoria hesitates, a pause that is known to even the strongest of us. Still, life depends on acquiescence, and she is nothing if not dutiful. Nevertheless, her hand rattles as she reaches for the knob and after, when she has surveyed the yard and let the cat out, when she again is sitting at the table, she has to prop the tips of her fingers together in a way that might for some resemble the spire of a church but to her is more two leans of fence. And then, some moments later, the cat comes back in, tail raised in happy greeting.

Astoria continues in that house, the one her grandparents built, for all of her life and a few months after. Years earlier, she had laid down the first carpet the house had known. At the same time, she painted each room blue to increase the flow of the whole; that is, all walls the same throughout: the color a carpenter may see in the world when he is ready to make his move, the color that penetrates his eyes on the long, long voyage to America in 1907, the color that changes everything and nothing at all.

Springer

He has forgotten where he is but is confident that he soon will recognize something. The sound of monks is melodious in the background, his dog attentive. Fear leaves him like a mail train; that is, he is aware some part of him has been taken away, snatched, but believes it is stowed safely enroute. That part of him moves smoothly down the line.

The boy's name is Springer, Springer Morris. He is not quick, barely as quick as his dog who was named after its breed: Springer.

"Where are we, boy?" he says softly, casually. The dog offers silent opinions which are never refuted. "We're OK, boy, we're OK." He ruffles the auburn hair. The sun is in the late sky, the heat hovers at its height and the sitting room is still but for dog, boy, and radio.

The monks stop, replaced by Brahms. The phone rings and boy and dog look up. It soon stops. The dog noses an edge of carpet and goes to retrieve the newspaper.

"Springer," Mrs. Morris calls as the dog returns, paper held high. "Dinner! Come on now."

Boy and dog regard each other, then follow her voice. One rubs his foot clean, one leaves the paper on the floor, one remembers he has forgotten to pee and one anticipates a simple happiness nearby.

A man wearing a suit of white tropical linen and a Panama hat steps onto a bus idling in a narrow stall where it has waited, seemingly, for him. Children at the rear of the bus make slapping sounds on the windows. In less than an hour the bus reaches the station at the edge of the city. He exits with a tip of his hat to the driver. Then he bends into a taxi waiting at a yellow stand. The engine makes tapping sounds under the hood. The taxi segment of the trip being the shortest, he soon arrives at the pier where sits a large white ship sailing today for Maui. Water makes lapping sounds at its sides.

Walking onto the pier he feels the breeze fill out his clothes, senses coolness on his ankles and wrists. The sun however, warms him, and as it does he looks up at it and is reminded of a mango or an orange. He checks the security of his hat on his head. At the other end of the pier, he can see ship stewards coming out on the deck and disappearing again through doorways as though drawn through a straw.

A woman arrives at the pier. Her sandals make clapping sounds on the wood. She sees a man in loose linens that wave gently on him. She stands near him for a minute and looks in the same direction as he does, at the large white ship. "Maui," she says aloud with a smile and a forward tip of her head. In case she has addressed him, the man acknowledges her pleasure. "Maui," he says. After another moment she moves on down the pier toward the ship. He stands as he was, savoring the weather.

A small group of children pour onto the pier from a yellow bus. They run excitedly by on either side of him. He briefly becomes the center of a sort of 'O' among them. A dog on its leash jumps and makes yapping sounds. More taxis, cars and people begin to arrive at the pier. Cameras emerge from cases, soft drinks spill, bits of litter lift in the breeze. Couples gesture and talk as they walk toward the ship. A woman pats her hair. Someone bumps the man's shoulder, apologizes, and moves on. The pier smells of popcorn and diesel. Activity and anticipation grow as passengers and crew prepare for departure.

Then, in a blur of flashing cameras and fluttering ticket stubs, voices wilt away and he sees that everyone else has moved far down the pier. A gap widens between well-wishers and passengers, the latter now filing up the gangway and onto the ship as though drawn through a straw. Water churns at the stern. The air fills with the sound of engines. The man in the Panama hat thinks *Maui* to himself and nods with satisfaction. The breeze plays with his hat. He smiles to himself, such as one may do at the end of a particularly well-performed symphony piece, then turns back toward the pavement and the yellow stand. He bends into a taxi and in a short while steps onto a bus. An hour or so later he resumes his bed. His mouth makes soft napping sounds in his sleep.

Once there were two sisters. One of them wore herself outside in, the other, inside out. In all other ways except age they were alike, as much as sisters can be alike, which is both a lot and not at all.

The one sister let everything she saw come in. She took everything in from outside. One day she said, "Today I am going to learn Greek" and she did. Another day she said, "I am going to become a classical musician. " Sometimes she took things in without comment: She bought a car; she had a baby. She didn't mention everything. Not, for instance, if she didn't think she was going to keep it very long.

The other took everything in, too, but could not use it in any practical way, so she took it in, thought about it, then looked for something she could have instead that was somewhat like it. She wore herself inside out. Soon she had a room filled with things she'd taken in and taken out again: aged icons, miniature amphorae, a machine to play the records she bought after hearing beautiful music, things from watching her sister and things that had nothing to do with her at all: a beautifully bound book of poems, a mouse.

Sometimes the sisters tried each other out. That is, they each tried to be their reverse. It didn't work very well. The meticulous one suddenly would not take care of her things. The other found she could not speak. Each way had required its special skills.

For fun, once, they tried just to be a little more like the other. At the end of the day they were half this, half that. Then they were frightened it might take both of them to make one. Then they were afraid there would be no one left to be a sister to. And then they were afraid they would die.

One day one of them did die. The outside-in one. She was lying in her bed thinking how she should go about dying, and then she did. The other one stared for a long time without moving or breathing. The doctor looked at the bed and said, "She's gone."

A minute or two later the inside-out one, who had been still for what seemed like a long time, took a very deep breath. This alarmed the doctor who turned to look at her. But as nothing further happened, he left.

When she too left the room, she was just her. She didn't know exactly what to do. She had taken in something but could not use it in any practical way. And then she was afraid she would die. And then she was afraid she would not.

The Waving Woman

East of the pier in a small neighborhood, a woman at the end of the street is waving to the postman who has just left mail at her porch. Or she is waving to the garbage man who emptied the cans, the gardener who tidied the neighbor's yard, or the musical woman a few doors down and her student who have finished their lesson. She makes this gesture so often, so ecumenically, it is difficult to tell for whom it is meant. None can remember her hands hanging still at her sides. She has waved, they say, to a bird, a cat, to trees in the daylight, to one or another star in the night.

Whoever notices her believes she is waving solely to them. For that moment they feel at home in the world and do not consider at all the disturbance she causes the air—the churn, the displacement as her hand cuts left then right. So much in life goes uncared for.

When the earthquake strikes Japan, mountains of water bearing citizens, cars, trees, street signs, buses, boats and small buildings roll out into the sea, carrying everything forward like gifts. When the tsunami reaches California it floods into the bay. As it approaches the little neighborhood east of the pier it notices something and hurries to meet it: the waving flag of dry land.

Polly, Pretty Polly

He wrote a song for the forest. Not of, but for. A song of gratitude, of manly affection and understanding. He presented it with pride and apprehension—should it not please, the mood be off or the song too simple, or in case the forest would fail to see him at all, standing there, who he was, singing.

He had to make his gift aloud. Paper would not do, nor bark, charcoal, or the pointed feathers fallen at wood's edge. He sang as if his lungs were outside of himself, as if feelings could fly out in a lasso of breath.

It is the same, always: the lost sing their love to the labyrinth and the wild swans of complication tie clouds to the notes, draping them on everything. And the water in the heart of the air rains where it will, equally on bush and fungus, on one bringing gifts. Today it is a soft rain, a glistening rain, a cooling comfort handed down by the leaves—an embrambling that may, though sweet, drown who would be comforted.

Sensing the last of his breath, the great trees bent toward the surface of his eyes to read what the soul would leave there. As they straightened, they sang quietly, *Polly, Pretty Polly*, remembering loss within their depths. Then they turned away to face where they were thickest and darkest, their movement causing a wind that made the smaller of them hum.

Tundra

Raahe, Finland, March, 2002: Seventy-year-old twin brothers have died within hours of one another after separate accidents on the same road in northern Finland, according to Police Officer Marja-Leena Huhtala. The first died when he was hit by a lorry while riding his bike in Raahe, 600 kilometers north of the capital, Helsinki. About two hours later, before police could notify the family, his brother crossed the same road on his bicycle and was also hit and killed by a lorry, 1.5 km from the spot where his brother died.

Traveling down the road a man careens into a truck and dies. Careening down another road, another. Blood is wax, a candle going home in shuttered dusk. Hands, like moths, flutter on the grass.

A man beside a lake evaporates. The sun is warm across his skin, and this will leave him, too. Winter hard, lake gone, the man is less and less the air than frost. He leans some leaves against himself, against the cold which rubs his heart. He speaks, a note too deep to sound. His stare precipitates the sky and to some extent the wind that skims the ox, the hare, the bleached cold feathers of the snowy owl, low as light.

Traveling down the road a man careens into himself. His brother rubs his heart with hands skinned thin. The sun evaporates. He leans some bones against himself. He leans some shrubs, some lichen, sedge, and moss. He leans some fish. Silence leaves his skin and turns his brother into air.

Traveling down a marsh, a lake, a bog, a stream, the months that warm are hard to find and then they turn and it is cold. Chill inhabits cells, as tight as wrens. A man can die and then his brother and the ground may freeze into its depths. Water sinks as low as it can go and then the sky is shut. Raw as casings.

Down the road a traveler. His soul is iced. Not a man to stop before a house, a door, a life. He rubs his hands to candles in his heart. He looks for gaps along a fence, a side way, low as light. His heat evaporates. He leans against a post. Lamps turn loose his features in the dusk. He sinks, the bleached cold feathers of the shuttered dark. Moths collapse against the glass. Absence rubs on absence like a thought.

Three Views

Clyde

He faces the water from a ledge. The ocean boils and roars in
its surge to the shore. The way he rocks on his heels when
buffeted by the wind shows him he is empty.

He came all the way to the coast from the Dust Bowl where
there is but one history for everyone: silt. As soon as they
stand upright, they are covered with it, filled, marked at surface
and depth by it; and also by rust, longing and the indelible
stains of crime.

He must lean into the gale in order to keep his feet. Needles
of seawater stab his face. A shock of air hits his fedora hard
and pushes at his vest. He steps forward as onto a running
board. Wind tears through him like a .38.

Durante

At the end of the program, when children already have gone
to their rooms and stored the day under the bed from where it
will ooze like oil into their dreams, Jimmy Durante turns to
glance at the audience and begins his walk upstage. He
balances an occasional over-the-shoulder look with his casual
striding away. He lifts his hat and sings goodnight to us,

goodnight to vaudeville, *goodnight, goodnight, goodnight,* and steps through a series of circular spotlights on the floor. Jimmy and his shoes of eclipse.

Between houses, at the curbside, passed by but few cars, a cat—this part black, this part white—surveys his situation then makes his way up the drive.

Ray

When he is alone and has put on his coat and hat to go outside, he sometimes believes he sees what looks like a shadow or a deep hole floating on the floor of the foyer—or on the porch or among the clustered asters at the front. He sees this in many places and when he does, he stops to gaze into it. Sometimes while gazing, he feels a small sort of motor start up in him.

At those times he knows the best thing for him is to keep looking because it might also happen that in the deep hole he will see a quick movement, possibly a fish, in which case he will want his tackle and net.

When he is alone and has stopped, he gazes, approaching happiness and staying with it a while—in a room, on a porch, on a beach, jetty, bank, or in a boat; one hand steering, one holding the line.

Columbus Day

One year a storm hit the city and was later named for the holiday that fell on that same day.

During the worst of it they improvised their dinner because the power had gone out. They talked late into the evening by the fireplace because there was no television, no radio and no light to read by and because they were excited and did not know what to expect.

When they tired of talking, they opened a bottle of red wine. Meanwhile, leaves, branches and paper blew all over the neighborhood, piling up against fences and porches and stopping up the storm drains. Shingles came loose, rain leaked under sills, trees fell. Animals hid and shivered, and some ran away.

On that day, in another year long before this, a man stood beside Columbus at the prow of the skiff. He saw the sun, the shore, the landing spot, the faces watching them from between the leaves of shore trees. He balanced on his two feet in a boat framed by sky and sea. Newness was nothing to him. He hoped there would not be any trouble.

Employing a practiced leveraging of wrist and elbow, her fingers reach to tip the book slightly away from the bookshelf, pausing, arm and hand angled in a manner similar to the pose of a praying mantis, then she brings up her other hand to steady the book and tease it from its place on the shelf. She is so attentive, she might be rotating the dials of a safe, listening to the tumblers.

The book, King-Helle's biography of Erasmus Darwin, needs her attention. A hanging chip on the spine of the dust jacket has become awkwardly askew under the protective covering she herself had applied. That attended to, she looks for other areas of concern, running a palm over the soft plastic to feel for new warping of the boards under the blue cloth of the book itself. She is thrilled at her power to stop attrition in its tracks.

She does not intend a thorough evaluation that day, beyond the obvious problems. Mostly she wants to check for mildew and foxing around the illustrated plates, as she has recently done with the Hurst & Company *Man's Place in Nature* by Huxley and Henry Fairfield Osborn's *From the Greeks to Darwin*—Volume 1 of "The Biological Series" from Scribners (first edition, second printing.) She sits for a moment to admire the prior owner's inscription and the signature of the famous doctor himself. The dustjacket bears the original price,

$35, and the list of prior books by the author—in this case only one, a significant biography of Shelley. Next comes the frontispiece where she sees old Erasmus Darwin himself, a photograph of the portrait by Joseph Wright of Derby. Next, the publishing details: MacMillan & Co., London, 1963. It is not an old volume, but hard to find in this condition. She tips her head and reflects, *a scarce one.*

As she once again gets to her feet, her eyes suddenly fly to the open space on the shelf. The gap fills her with panic, even though she knows that what is missing is in her hands. A chill starts in her feet, nonetheless. It moves up her legs like damp, then up her spine toward her heart, leaching away all pleasure and well-being on its way. She sees in the emptiness a terrifying geometry of doors opening onto nothing except more and more opening doors. Shaken, she raises the book toward the vacancy and shoots it home like a bolt.

They were walking to a movie. "We're lucky," they'd said to their friends, "to live so close, to be able to walk there." It was evening when they started, then evening began to darken, first in the streets below the buildings then in the sky.

They were side by side in their coats, the long coats they chose for walking. The air was dark and thick. The thickness was a fog. They leaned into their stride, pushing fog aside and walking through it. Her collar was up against her neck. His scarf and hat nearly met. Chill rubbed on her legs. The circle of what they saw moved with them. Fog made what they saw larger.

A cigarette flared ahead of them. "Move farther out," she whispered. He took her arm and eased closer to the street. The fog left eddies behind them.

In a window, a pull-cord dangled, an empty ring at the end. He asked, "What time is it?"

"We're fine," she said.

The air was wet. It sat on their lashes, their cheeks, the tops of their shoes. It swallowed the street behind them. She said,

"I could use a cigarette." He leaned forward, the brim of his hat parting the fog. "Pretty close now," he said.

They passed a car splashed with neon. The seats were worn, the backs split. He asked, "Are you warm enough?"

They were walking to a movie. They lived nearby and were able to walk there. It was evening, there was fog. The air was dark and thick. They were side by side in their coats, the long coats they chose for walking. They believed they were nearly there. They had come to where they should have seen it. Had it not been for the fog, they'd have seen it long before.

Pension Anna

It was hot where they were and they were unable to bear it. The air that had nourished their animal blood so faithfully now paused at the ledge of their survival and would not jump.

It was hot where they were, inside and outside the same. As if hot were offered as meals. As if hot were the sleeve of the route to *Pension Anna.*

When they arrived at the inn, greetings swelled out to them and doormen of various heights moved quickly, opening and closing the doors of commerce. They had reserved rooms. They'd brought with them their valise of describable deeds. They were tended to by staff; mostly they kept to themselves, covering the mirrors and vases with towels. Things that they generally thought of when they regarded themselves flowed and ebbed in their minds, now pooled with new thoughts of the weather which, in that particular place, was moderate. *Welcome to Pension Anna.*

They were kept like small animals and herded ever more toward a center—the ballroom of limited choice—and stayed longer than they could have imagined, the concierge, familiar and filled with mirth, showing, rewinding, and showing them films of interminable loss.

*The Silence of Galleries,
Voices of Objects*

The Silence of Galleries, Voices of Objects

More than an hour south of sprawling metropolitan Seattle, Washington, is the Olympia estate of a man who made his fortune in the early Pacific Northwest by milling flour. His mill, built 100 years ago, was a symbol of industrial expansion in the young state which only twelve years prior had still been a Territory. The owner of the business was fair and just—in his era he might have been called "stalwart," his offspring, "steady." The enterprise succeeded handsomely, eventually allowing him to build a manor house on an expanse of property overlooking Puget Sound. The home comprised a sufficient number of rooms which, along with supporting cottages, housed not only the core family but all the extended family on the country's western coast. Over time, with quiet elegance verging on anonymity, the forward-looking members of this family helped their young city grow—donating to civic causes, founding an opera, supporting a university. They attracted so little attention that the townspeople did not bother to manufacture scandals or examples of meanness to hang on them; goodness often a bore to so many. The family was long-lived, their children well-behaved, and their social presence— though fundamental to the town that had grown to become the state capital—remained tastefully inconspicuous.

The more than ten floors of the old mill and many silos are stilled now, decaying for decades, giving themselves over to the wet, rust and mold endemic to northern coastal climes, but a small coterie of remaining family still occupies and maintains the estate. For the last several years they have encouraged visitors to visit an area of their home where, in dedicated display rooms, they may view an array of treasured family belongings—the urge to share still great. It is their last gift to the public who has for long—and perhaps this next word is not too strong—revered them. It is an uncharac-teristically public gesture, only thinkable now that the extant family has dwindled to a few whose nature and age keep them from overt social activities and because, presumably elsewhere on the grounds, they have found—as must we all—a place to hide.

*

1. *The Seth Thomas Metronome*

Entering the first display room of the manor, one encounters the pyramidal shape of a metronome that sits on a copper tray beside a small figurine depicting the young Tutankhamun about to spear a fish. Designed to provide the rhythms to guide a performer through musical measures, the metronome is all that remains of family evenings of entertainment for which a player, now long-since passed, practiced at the piano. She had only to remove the faceplate from the metronome and press the counting wand to release Time from its coiled, motionless silence.

2. *Verticality*

Opposite the metronome, at the end of a narrow table, sits a monocular, an object the same in shape and function as binoculars, but halved. A handwritten note indicates it was a gift from the parents to their eldest son on his tenth birthday. How puzzled he may have been, after his initial excitement, to contemplate an object most notable for what isn't there. His friends had the usual binoculars, and he wondered if the gift, though unique, represented a generosity partially withheld? A hint that his prospects in life would be less than he had hoped? An implication that he, like the non-stereoptic rabbit or goldfish, would never see completely all that lay before him? Or might it mean that he was celebrated by only one of his parents? Soon he was so filled with thoughts about *completion* that he had to write them down.

Next to the monocular, in the center of the table, rests an open clarinet case, each of the black wood sections of the instrument standing upright in the case rather than lying horizontal in their fitted deep blue velvet nests or joined together for playing. The bottom section sits on its flared bell, the mouthpiece stands on its cork joint and tapers skyward. Together with the remaining sections—barrel, upper, lower joint—all struggling to stay vertical on the uneven, soft lining, they comprise an old-growth woodland of potential music, nickel keys shining like the moon.

Immediately to the right of the case are five reproductions of totem poles. Faithful copies of the Haida argillite carvings (which were themselves small stone objects rather than the familiar tall wooden poles), these black resin figures, like the originals, celebrate myths, families and the unsayable—depictions, like sound, able to summon the deep. Their similarity in appearance to the uprights in the clarinet case makes one want to scoop them up and integrate them into the adjacent blue forest. The daily disarrangement of the poles on the table suggests some visitors attempt to do so.

3. *The Bust of Charles Darwin*

Old photos by the door reveal that the bust of Charles Darwin was not originally placed within the breakfront bookcase. It first occupied one end of the drinks bar, then graced a small hand-painted table depicting the South American *Leopardus pardalis*, the ocelot. Now on a shelf in the bookcase nearest the window, the bust rests between Darwin's *Forms of Flowers*, third edition, and the two-volume *Animals and Plants;* the expensive first editions having been sold years before. This Darwin—for the sculpture memorializes not the full-bearded old scholar but the young man—would surely have never anticipated the impact of what he would achieve.

The oldest son of the family would sometimes sit in the chair by the window in this room, when damp mornings kept him inside, and watch the mist begin to accumulate on the window and eventually form drops that merged with other drops, growing bigger and heavier until they sagged and ran down the glass with others like them in wavy wet lines that formed a kind of curtain.

4. A Wooden Carving of the Wind

An example of woodcarving done by the indigenous people of southeastern Alaska is displayed upon what the family called *the ocelot table*. Carved into the foot-tall piece of yellow cedar is a round face with closed eyes and puffed cheeks and a smaller, deeper circle: a round mouth from which one can imagine the sound of blowing wind, wind that might bring a canoe toward the shore or push it farther out to sea. The family believed the piece represented the origin of the wind itself which, once it emerged from confinement, spread and moderated and filled every vacant space. At that point it became so sovereign, so omnipresent, that the word for both its nature and its world would be the same: Air inhabits the air.

Near this table, in a section of the room devoted to modern art, stands a bisque statue of a man, eight-inches tall, painted various shades of blue and gray. As it is with bisque, all water has been fired from the clay resulting in a light and fragile form. Named Wind Man by the artist some forty years ago at Lake Garda, the ceramic coat and hair sweep to one side as if blown by the wind. Painted on his chest is a round moon, his only anchor in turbulence. Somehow Wind Man survived the arduous transport by train and long flight from Italy to its current home. Here it stands, where it was placed decades ago, precarious on clay feet, facing each force and withstanding it.

5. *The Signet-Shaped Gouge*

The breakfront bookcase by the window is perhaps the oldest of the family's furnishings, acquired on one of many trips abroad. Two pulls are missing, and there is a small, curved gouge on the horizontal shelf atop the drawers. If the family ever noticed it, they did not repair it. The angle and position of the damage suggests the impact of a heavy object or an emphatic fist, whose signet ring has rotated around the finger and become the point of impact. Fortunately, the damage is visible only close up though once seen, the speculation it invites is unsettling.

6. *Six Framed Engravings by Tiepolo*

Facing a short wall in this room, one thinks: *This family surely spent time in northern Italy,* for that is where one falls in love with Tiepolo. A true love this must have been, resulting in the 1908 purchase and framing of a number of engravings by the famous Venetian, Giovanni Domenico Tiepolo, eldest son of the eighteenth-century family of artists and the most realistic of them in artistic style. Arranged horizontally above a dark wooden bench, the engravings are true masterworks.

The first in the series is a landscape. In this, as usual, Tiepolo has structured his pictorial elements in the manner of theater stage design, placing a camel in the background to convey a desertscape, adding a walled town here, an apprehensive shepherd there, and, as he did in the next four pieces, employing a snail's-eye perspective to dramatize persevering travelers.

In the sixth work, we see an old man sitting at a table. He is framed by a window through which he could see dramatic scenes were he but to look up. He has been told, we are given to know by another figure gesturing urgently, that he must arise and flee. Ignoring the warning, our subject remains in his chair. Vapor rises from a cup before him. His actions are small: He glances toward a reliquary. He touches his ring.

This last of the Tiepolos is the only one to depict an indoor scene. Only after regarding this engraving does one realize that, of all the art displayed in the room, each except this is a landscape. A card at the end of the bench states that this single picture was purchased by the family patriarch on a second excursion undertaken during a period of personal and worldwide turmoil some three decades after acquiring the other five.

7. *A Painting of Portuguese Olive Trees*

Were a guest to tour this room at a particular time of day, when evening beckons the heart toward its home, he or she might notice out of the corner of the eye a small-bodied, long-legged spider moving fast across the wall, looking at first like a blown ball of fluff, then disappearing behind the painting *Portuguese Hills* (the title we learn from a small card slipped into the corner of the frame). Will the spider stay behind the painting or suddenly emerge to race along another route? Eventually one's thoughts move on to the painting itself.

Recipient of an honorable mention for this work in a juried show, the artist has painted a grove of olive trees casting shadows across bronze-colored ground. Evidence of this species of tree has been found on the Iberian Peninsula as early as the Bronze Age, and indeed it is not possible to say whether this painting purports to show the ancient trees of Portugal or those more recent. And since olive trees are evergreen, it is also impossible to tell with certainty the season, though it would be enjoyable to think it is summer. Studying the shade, and assigning (rightly or wrongly) compass north to the top, one may decide the piece depicts summer, at eight o'clock PM. The trees are full, and though the painted sun still floods most of the picture it does not penetrate the leaves to reveal the branches, flowers, or fruit. The viewer must imagine those. In the elongate shadows the artist shows us the frustrations of light, the depth and reach of its absence.

The artist, in the unending pursuit of perfection, seems to have added more earth-colored paint between two already finished trees in hopes of correcting or enhancing an effect. The effort was unsuccessful. For some viewers, it may be hard not to return again and again to this troublesome area, forsaking the rest; hard not to speculate on the inadequacy that caused this afterthought, also inadequate. Hard, too, not to wonder about the spider. Other viewers will overlook these distractions and simply focus on the resonant colors of the grove and on the intimations, in the silvery-green leaves, of delicious olives and warm, honied evenings filled with wine and music and the promise of a pleasant turn, later, in light summer clothes, through an immaculate courtyard.

Leaving the picture and this room, visitors enter a hallway where they see an exit sign pointing to a door with small windows of colored glass that will take them to the outside lawns. They are excited to see what the sun has to show them.

8. *Five Thirty-Eight*

Exiting the manor to the yard, guests find a welcoming assortment of benches and chairs that face well-tended gardens and walkways. Here they might rest awhile and enjoy views the family once contemplated through their windows: soft pink rhododendrons lining a pathway into the aspens, a collection of succulents and hostas punctuated by smooth gray stones, a great expanse of lush green grass, and, in the middle of the lawn, dozens of miniature roses surrounding the basin of a fountain burbling water into the pool below.

The eldest son of the family had become old enough to consider his adulthood and how it might evolve, though he had yet to achieve his majority and financial freedom. His dream was to become an architect. From his bedroom window, using the monocular he received on his birthday years ago, he could daily admire one particular building beyond their grounds. With its sleek lines and geometric details, it was a fine example of Art Deco style. Its stucco finish and rounded corners, so different from his own house, sang out to him. He was fascinated by the chevrons of mosaic tiles and the way a section of the front appeared to be stepped back from the façade. He imagined the door would bear a sunburst of stained glass in its upper half and, lower, a long door handle set vertically. He further imagined a mural in the hall or dining room and angular chrome and glass light fixtures throughout. A paragon of a house! Though he had never met or even seen the people living there, he thought they must be as stylish as the house, perhaps even glamorous. He was falling in love with the house next door. It became his focus, and he invested in it his hopes for the life of perfection he believed could be his.

One day he went, as was his habit, to his door to retrieve the mail. He waved cheerfully toward the departing postal truck. There was nothing delivered for him that day, but one letter was misdelivered—addressed to that fascinating house number 538 rather than his own 554. He paused for a moment to consider his potential for boldness, then set out to deliver the letter himself and so get an up-close view of his ideal.

The front of 538 was as he had imagined, and he hurried up the front walk to see more. He found the door ajar but could hear no sounds inside. He realized that if he leaned forward, he would be able to see into the entryway and partway into the living room. His eyes were slow to focus, coming out of the bright sunlight, but he soon noticed serious shortcomings: the paint was in an appalling condition—stained and faded, chipped—and several floor tiles had been cracked long ago and not repaired. Grunge divided the pieces. The ceiling lights were modern, tasteless disks of plastic. What furniture he saw was undistinguished, worn and dirty. The air inside was sepulchral with mold, overlain with food smells.

He decided not to knock. He placed the letter on sill of the entry and stepped off the porch. He walked rapidly back to his house without a glance behind him. Back in his own room, he pulled the blinds, put his monocular in the closet and sat down on the edge of the bed. Day after day he stayed in his room as much as possible, not reading or listening to music but sitting, looking at the floor, sometimes lying down with his eyes closed. He fell into a melancholy which deepened until nothing was able to lift him.

Two years later an uncle died, leaving him some money. The young man obtained a passport and set off to Europe on a trip of such duration and mystery that we know nothing further about him.

9. *An Operations Manager*

Over the years, members of the family moved away from the manor house and not a few of them died. The master plan, starting with the father, always had included the display rooms. After the father passed away, the mother took the reins until she became too hobbled and muddled. The eldest son had disappeared abroad, so the responsibility fell to the second son, and so on, eventually, resting on the youngest daughter, the last known surviving family member, who only recently had reached the age at which she could inherit.

For a few years she managed everything by herself—the displays as well as her own life. The distraction of so much work proved a help in her solitude and grief at the loss of her last sibling. As time went on, however, she realized she would benefit greatly from engaging someone to help her. She hired a young man to maintain the house, organize the housecleaners and groundskeepers, and manage the public rooms. He was slightly young, she thought, but he proved to be conscientious. He enjoyed his work, and she was very pleased.

Three decades passed, during which this arrangement worked well for both her and the Operations Manager, as she called him. Each year, on the anniversary of his date of hire, they would meet in the study. He would tell her how things stood with the displays—how many people had come to see them, what, if anything, needed to be changed or improved or rearranged, whether the walls needed repainting, and so on. She would sit at her father's desk and listen. When he finished, she would open the ledger, make the required entry and notations, and write a check paying him in advance for the upcoming year. Then she would close the ledger and hand him the check with a word or two of thanks. They each looked forward to this little ceremony that remembered a year now gone and heralded a year to come.

As might be expected, infirmity slowly crept upon her, one ailment at a time. She long ago had stopped visiting the display rooms. It made her sad to look upon the beloved items, sad to conjure her dead family in this way. When the Operations Manager called to say an artifact had broken, as could reasonably happen, or disappeared altogether, and to ask what she would like done, her reply was pleasant, but invariable: "Do what you think is best." In some ways, the Operations Manager felt those rooms displayed his own life, too, he had been so long in complete charge of them.

Life at the house continued. Visitors wrote to say they enjoyed their time spent with the family history and in the gardens. She was happy to share both. She appreciated the careful efficiency of the Operations Manager, and he appreciated the free hand he was given in his work as well as the financial arrangement that suited them both.

During her eighth decade, she began to worry about the effects of aging on her mind. She sometimes forgot appointments, occasionally lost things and at times was bewildered to recall what she had just set out to do. The Operations Manager was aging too, though, to her, he seemed sure of himself and did not appear to be slowing down at all. For his part, he did worry that one day she might sell the house. He did not think she was well and, although he was not anxious about his own future, he did wonder what would become of the artifacts.

One day she was driving around her old haunts—the neighborhood surrounding the local university she had attended. She felt nostalgic that day, enjoying seeing the old landmarks, searching in vain for favorite restaurants, pointing out to herself buildings where friends had lived and parks where they had picnicked together. After a few unexpected turns on street newly made one-way only and more than one detour for roadwork, she realized she did not recognize any of the buildings around her. She did not know exactly where she was and could not see the small lettering on the street signs. She began to panic—which road led where, which would see her home. Once again, she felt the pain in her side, one she had felt before, and as she tried to loosen her seatbelt which had cinched tightly about her, her desperation to get home grew.

Eventually, she happened onto the road she needed for escape but the cumulative effect of the day had been exhausting. Back in her house, she skipped afternoon tea and lay down for a nap.

The next day was the annual ritual with the Operations Manager. She entered the study and sat down at the desk. He had been waiting a few minutes for her and noticed that her hair was untidy. Her eyes did not meet his as he gave his account of things, and she only nodded absently before opening the ledger. She took a deep breath then straightened abruptly before exhaling. He saw that, and saw the hesitation to pick up the pen, and in that pause, it occurred to him to ask whether she might think it better, more prudent, since he was getting on in years, to engage him on a month-to-month basis rather than pay the whole year ahead. She considered this idea as she made her entry and wrote out his check. She stood slowly and said, "No, but thank you. No changes." She handed him the check. "The self is a tender animal, my friend."

Field Notes

A Series of Questions

Deciding to start with a series of questions; and to do this in appropriate circumstance, I prepare the items for inquiry: a bird, his bright palimpsest announcing the extent of his house from a branch; his tree, not as colorful but sharing a leveling absence of address; the sun.

A common medium for announcement is papyrus or linen. The tree is ginkgo, the sound, finch.

Sun anoints the bird, tumbles the length of the tree, encircles the shadows they combine to make, steps in through the window and lies down on my desk.

An untidiness of thin white rectangles is being loved by the sun on my desk, passions flashing before my eyes. The proper piece of paper is selected. Left aside, things that need response: a transubstantiated email, requests for payment. Other sheets glare blankly or curl as if to tap my shoulder. Something is owed there, too.

I choose paper with an amoebic splash of coffee. Separated from its brother, another bears a ring of the same color—in disorder, larger chaos. Such hallmarks call to me. I will take up where these have been put down.

The window is partly raised, permitting a fresh Easter kind of air. Crumpled pages rotate in the bin like sharks. Such tools of circulation make and erase the film of the day before, the weeks, the months, the camera. The age of imprecision all equal, I aim to connect epiphanies.

I drop the window a third. Ease should be easily had, and the window is smooth in the casement, a tribute to manufacturing—my success with it a matter of leverage. The remaining open window space is sorted by wisteria. A cottony leaf pokes in like a saddle tramp and leans against a post.

A word instead of *leverage* is *charm*, perhaps *yellow*. I charmed the window partway. Wisteria wrote its name in foreshortened books. *Butter.* A word in place of *book* is *green*. A hanging blue ruffles like a rabbit's nose.

My chair is linked to the desk by my sitting in it—a sort of "bridge effect" of settlement, the merging forms of continent. We adjust these worlds by hops and by selecting a space for arms. I also must more seriously consider pens, but not just now—the aromas of breakfast rise like sun-bleached trains. The tracks need mending; the locomotives are lucky if they get through. It is time for me also to move ahead.

An overnighting fly wakes up and moves to a higher plane where he works an inscrutable outlook.

Lower in the jungle something may be possible.

Details attended, there remains but sage and trail.

1. How by path?
   Fjord?
2. The chaparral (greens and purples)
3. Sea

The Hunterian Museum

Illimitable Blue

Occasionally, the public is admitted in small numbers to an otherwise closed exhibit in the museum. Inside, they file in silently and allow themselves to be grouped in the center of the room where they arrange their feet by small movements to avoid others, square and straighten their shoulders under coats, roll the cloth of their umbrellas tight, easing the points carefully down a leg to the floor.

The doors are sealed, the room darkened. At a signal the ceiling rolls back and the room floods with light. They all look up at once to see a vision of the sky unlike any they have seen before. The room floods with an illimitable blue! It excites in them a rhapsody, a waterfall of sensation. They can scarcely control their hands. No one uses the words of anyone else to describe it. Their ecstasies tumble like the rich procession of the equinoxes.

After, as the sky is closing, they hear from outside, from a fathomable distance in the encrusted snow, a leaf crack underfoot. The snow magnifies it. It is indistinguishable from gunshot. The sound leaps into the room and bounces wall to wall. No one has the least idea how to say what has happened.

There, across this room, is something unexpected. We enter and lose ourselves within *The Dental Arcade*. Surrounded by seamless museum music and socketed light, *son et lumiere*, we find much to consider and discuss: incisors, canines, molars (the desire to return, which never goes away); enamel, dentine, cementum (such a pretty place is Cortina); worn, uneven crowns (they do the work that is the hardest in us all); pulp and base (and with a pretty church); fractures (simple as the rain); the eminences upon which the condyles imagine actions of the bone (the unsent letters of unspent passion).

And then an attendant, who has been otherwise busy on some business of his own, suddenly pulls the blinds from a large-windowed wall. We feel a rush and hear the clap of hands. The sight takes us right out of ourselves.

Ah! The *Dolomiti*, so much closer than we'd thought! Ridged, arched and cusped, pushed up by the jaw of firmament that powered, willed itself to erupt them. We feel the size, the violence as, ragged from their beds, they reached upward to consume the sky. How they seem to rise even more, as if to leave us; how our hearts would hold them. How we long for nothing other than to wake one day, braced with the crisp air of dawn, and climb them.

In The Shell Room, under bright lights, we read, *Shells cluster at a log, a rise, a rock, where water is impeded. Where reach exceeds hold, retreat is thwarted, and return stopped.* Here are thwarted limpets, augers, clams, moon snails curled in patterned sleep; here attendant nests, a depositional fan—collections in collections, seas in seas, longings of the trapped flotsam (the emptiest most frequent, the need to point this out, poignant.) Here the larger, smaller, tinier, the grace within debris, both high and drifted down, the afterthought of tide deflated then held as if by pins.

A clock chimes. Visitors are alert to change, the small alarms of time, and by instruction. Pulled by that which waits for them, they gather up their small packages, their dawdling children, and leave the way they came, the lights of the displays no longer beating on their necks.

We are meant to let our attention be drawn, within the glass enclosure of the museum case which houses the drawings by Albinus, to a particularly elegant and august man—the stature (how he lounges afoot, languid, an arm raised as to declare ... some observation or appraisal.) And the tree that stands nearby and seems to reach for him. And, above him, the cloak that seems to want to protect him and *yes, you see it there*, the proud, clear articulation: the intricate aqueduct of the spine. Atop it, *yes*, the skull. It is all just right, the angles of address, the hinges.

Our minds fill in for us the branching veins, the flow of air around the bones, the love the air has for its little trails. We inhale as we imagine he once did and see a breathing forest in his chest—a path, a hill, and out of sight, a river crossing, perhaps a rock, a bear, a salmon—accordions of air, the surges and withdrawals of life.

The skeleton is all confidence in its pose, as is that which flies above and that which flew away (the desire to climb and speak …) but *wait, look closely*, note the work by the craftsman who encased the image, who pieced together the glass frame, *look*, the delicate cornerings (*all remark on them*), the precision of the dovetails, the wooden bracings so strong yet careful and, somehow, the tender containment. *How he fit it so!*

At evening, after closing, the sketches are draped as if for sleep—a cloth of necessary grace. The tree of after-life is stilled, its leaves quieted, as is the skeletal stem, offering no visible clues for those who perhaps knew the man.

Because, it has been said, there was a figure—slight, hungry— who had long been walking and inquiring and who, approaching this place at night, long ago, tired almost beyond hope, looked up through the windows and across to the cases and felt he recognized … was just about to reach out and … was just about to cry out … *oh, it was a child!* He had traveled what seemed an eternity from the village, his heart within his hands, wanting only this: to follow him who stands before us now. And so there is a shade.

The Cataract

The policeman knows it is the scheduled time for walking up and down the street and rounding corners. He knows, but waits. Cold from the sidewalk climbs the statuary of his legs. For both a short time and eternity he stands in the alcove of the building, face up and outward, feeling for the first warm rays of morning.

Finally, a day begins. Light splashes the portico. His back against the bricks, he acknowledges recurring warmth—just as, at the rock-cut façade of Abu Simbel, above the cornice, does *Papio* raise stone hands to welcome the sun god *Ra*, who each day finds a way to defeat the gods of darkness.

Art Deco (The Pavilion)

A man stands on the veranda. The veranda is grand and white and beautiful and people at the party inside call it a pavilion, though it is not. They look out to the beautiful veranda and see a man looking out from a pavilion. They believe they are thinking of the view and not of the sea.

The veranda has vertical pieces where a hand might rest and a peak of beams and glass. Below is lattice. Everything complicates itself, up and down.

Through the outlook is the night, divided into sky and sea. The night sky and sea at night are so beautiful that verandas overlooking them may be pavilions. All the colors in the sky and the sea are blue—lapis, peacock, marine and blue so blue as to be black.

The party guests hold glasses shaped like diamonds. They look up as a man arrives and some of them say, "Oh!" or "There you are!" One says, "I'm mixing another batch!" The man sits down beside a woman with a sharp chin. He says, "May I?" She crosses her legs and leans and says, "Possibly," and someone else laughs.

The laughter is as sharp as her chin, as the points her knees make, as the angles of their glasses, the tip of the pavilion, the fumes of the gin in a new batch. The man flourishes his handkerchief. "A Houdini!" someone says. The man dabs at the corners of his eyes.

The woman watches him and thinks, *such beautiful blue eyes*, then looks away toward the wall of glass and the veranda. She rises, crosses the room, and goes outside.

A man stands on the veranda. He feels it is a pavilion, but it is not, though it is beautiful. People inside see a man looking out from a pavilion. They believe they are thinking of the view. The woman steps out and joins him. His cigarette responds to a breeze, his fingers hook lattice. She leans against him, light as a sheet. All the colors in the sky and the sea are blue.

Im Zoologischen Garten

Tell me something beautiful about the Steppes.

That they are the best tank fields in the world: unused. Green is brighter and colder there. Standing will feel like this: two strings vibrating toward one string vibrating. Grass and the burnishing air live on the tears of Steppe ponies. Everything is all and in itself and forgets to keep growing. You do not see this unless you are a khan. You hear it, hear how it is being, it is being *not more*. Hooves on the rocks ring like monasteries. The smaller bell of your soul writhes, a loose paper. Everything (your encampment) leans as if it would breathe. Breathing is reserved. It comes from beautiful swift ponies bending the wind around them.

They are Swiss and they are bears; accustomed to a cinch of mountains, they may not mind a cage.

Bern bears go in a circle left, go in a circle right. The Swiss levitate on observation decks and go in lines right, go in lines right, go in lines right. No matter that Bern bears are no longer there, the Swiss must look at them—the smooth turnings, the subtleties of their browns and how they rise on their feet at just the right moment. This is where one can look directly. The

mountains hide everything else. In Bern it can be managed.
Look, Oma, a lake of bears!

Half a snow monkey.

He watches them bathe. Many years he has watched them. He
is not excited. He watches people fade to steam in the hot
pools of Shiga Kogen, watches steam curl at their ears and hide
their bodies. He sees steam faces, steam people.

The second half of his secret: Afterward, he, too, bathes. Wet
monkey by moon in Shiga Kogen. Steam curls at his ears and
hides his body. He dunks, he shakes, he stands up in the water.
See! Half a snow monkey!

Concessions

A ticket to the zoological garden does not include a ticket to
the botanical garden. It is *non compris*. The concession stand is
at the margin of the garden. It is before the low gate where
you must pay to go farther. Beyond the concession stand, over
the head of the man with your spun sugar, your glazed apple,
over the umbrella above his head, you see the structure
containing the botanical exhibit. Its panes of glass flash as the
sun moves across them, like the lens of a man's eyeglasses
which, when they are turned toward you, give a momentary

light. Before, you have seen only pictures of it: pictures of soaring glass with surprising angles that veer away like birds; lush courtyards and huge doors and uncountable pieces of wood holding it all together, wood cut into all possible sizes to hold together the uncountable glass squares that make up the walls and ceiling and even the doors of the botanical garden, wood like the stalks and trunks that grow in great numbers inside. It is all of a piece: house of glass and house of wood. What a sad, empty sound it would be if a rock broke one of the panes of glass. What a great and beautiful sound it would be if a fire burned the botanical garden altogether, burned and weakened the wood until it could no longer support the uncountable glass panes, so they all fell at once but in their own ways, some of them cracking, some of them crashing and splintering, some of them tinkling softly to the ground like spun sugar. What a beautiful sound that would be.

In Hartmann Hall

Normally the Salle Hartmann is used for boxing and wrestling matches, occasionally ballet, but the advance scouts of sound technicians have declared it also ideal for symphony recordings, its many wooden surfaces reflecting deliciously both timbre and texture. The soundmen themselves are not particularly fond of music but they do like perfection.

During the Bach *Concerto for Two Violins in D minor*, through a window open to the Mainzerstrasse Allee, trucks stacked full of office supplies can be heard accelerating through various gears as they enter traffic. They are in the recording, too, but the conductor has his own ideals of perfection and hears only his players. He shushes and encourages, lost in his ears, as dedicated as a bat. When he lifts his head his baton lifts with it; also his glance, inclusive.

*

Small birds light on the scroll of the Third Violin who is third for a reason which he accepts, his heart light and feathery in supporting passages. His name is Edgar. His father is a baker of the type of doughnuts that emerge from ovens in twists. His mother died young. He pauses for the birds, reading the score silently. Occasionally his eyes rest peacefully on the breasts of the Second Violin.

Erika, for her part, is unaware of the stare of her neighbor and anyway does not regard herself as a vision of rapture. She knows her part in the piece but not yet her heart. Her eyes are wide, her thoughts elsewhere—the participation of elements always unsure and a bit uneven. Her head is turned a little, her eyebrows lifted. Her makeup is thick as paint, yet she is rural, born on an asparagus farm outside the city. In a dream, she turns a page and prepares. She is as ready as the hardy crowns of the crop are for harvest—now more than two years old, their roots deep in the sandy loam. She draws her bow quickly across the strings. A cut is made against the green, near the base, at a steep angle.

*

Ingrid, page-turner for the pianists, has no duties. She doesn't know why she was asked to come in. A piano is not even in this piece. She hovers at the curtain behind which are stored exercise weights. It must be somehow her fault, this lack of assignment, she supposes—pleasures so hard to come by, guilt easily had, defeat (though complex) easier still. (No sooner had she stopped antacids, for instance, then she took up breaded fish.)

After an interval, the orchestra resumes its seats, not one of the members aware that Ingrid has been absent by then the length of time it takes to cover three miles (west) on foot, craning her neck this way and that for the sun—the light exciting her glasses, perspiration patrolling her skin as she

looks down and counts out her coins at the entrance to The
Succulent Gardens.

*

The second half of the recording is Ravel's *Bolero*. The
characteristic of the piece is amplification within repetition,
though a straightforward beauty may be vast and powerful
and the composition in its heart aims for all that. The small
orchestra is wrapped in the arms of the elevated sports ring,
now used as a soundstage, no one thinking to clear the space
of canvas, ropes, buckles, buckets, towels. The conductor
stands lower than the players, on the exercise floor, his baton
atop the mast of his arm. He has spatial disadvantage. During
the performance, he is tense. Boards creak, sweat seeps into
air. He does not like the piece but has prepared for it and
now he leans into it, attuned to ever-tinier bits, only to be
jolted by strengths he'd notated but had underestimated.
Small as they are, these sharp silicates of sound multiply and
join forces and fling themselves right at him in surprising and
fearful shapes. As if jabbing and swinging, their increasing
power begins to eclipse him. As the piece goes on and on,
well beyond his powers to control it, his eyes, which earlier
had been facts, become loose interpretations or, shockingly,
only intent; two dwindling, powerless targets.

Everything moves toward destination, and all music toward
the conductor, the home of what it means to create. But this
music keeps throwing itself at him, a violence of the air. It

lands like burning comets, like the missiles of brave new countries, like massive and repeating floods of the ice age scraping the land bare. The notes rise in great coils and land on him, one after pitiless other.

His image shreds. He would duck, but his knees have locked. He would stop altogether, if only to retrieve the sheets dropping like hope from the stand, but he cannot. Nor can he scream out his terror, erased as he is by topping seas, now by bottomless deeps, now torn open with his insides scattered across a desert floor. Nor can he even turn or, at the last, to tell his family he loves them; nor separate his mind from sound, sound from place, place from traveler, traveler from the sights that overwhelm—the shattering sands so relentless against the legs.

Potlatch

Some have wrapped themselves in cloaks fastened by buttons.

There follows the giving of blankets or canoes or the breaking
of large copper plates engraved with the animal crests of their
owners.

The Mohs scale, developed c.1912, is used to compare the hardness of substances. Enamel falls between five (Apatite) and eight (Topaz.) Copper is soft.

At the feast, the host sings a scathing song ridiculing his rivals. Grease from the candlefish is passed in large spoons to the guests—first to the rival chief who, if he feels he has given a greater feast in the past, may refuse and run out of the house.

It is just right.

Day 1:

Pointing Figure is the wooden portrait of a man wearing a hat, made sometime between 1890 and 1900 for a group of brothers belonging to Raven Bone House of the Raven clan. An earlier *Pointing Figure* was set up on Cat Island by ancestors of the same group in honor of a deceased relative.

Andy Moses helped with the carving of this memorial but never inquired into the story behind it, since he was a young man and, like many young men, uninterested in such matters.

Day 2:

At the top of this pole is Raven with outspread wings. On his breast are three figures: the Children of the Sun, whom Raven visited during the Deluge. His wings are decorated with eyes within which are small faces that, in their carving traditions, symbolize joints as well as his power to change forms.

Day 3:

Only the man at the base of this pole could be salvaged from the elements. No photograph of the original exists. He has weathered to soft silver, reflecting the name of the pole, *Spirit of Hazy Island.* The pole conveys the lesson that misfortune comes to the frivolous and from such people the spirit withdraws its protections: their hair arches in the wind and drapes across their eyes; water stops reflecting them; the sky hides from them within the trees, and the clouds above them drop right down to the ground. Such people are in danger of losing their lives.

Day 4:

Usually, details such as eyebrows and ears are omitted in these representations of inanimate objects.

Day 5:

Flicker-wing feathers ornament this headdress that has a carved wood plaque in front and weasel skins hanging down the back.

In December the sun arcs above the horizon like a stone in the long portion of a skipped rock.

Day 6:

Use of the leg as a primary design feature is unusual. Most often the whole body is depicted, though distorted and rearranged according to highly formalized conventions.

Electrons that create auroras start in the outer layers of the magnetic field, which is compressed by solar wind.

Day 7:

To distinguish symbolic images of wolf from bear, the carver may add a long, jointed tail to the wolf.

One type of Borealis is called a *corona*, the other a *band* or *curtain*. Pinwheels, drapes, arches, tints, ripples, points, swaths—after several minutes, everything fades into a warm green glow.

Day 8:

Aurora was the Roman goddess of the dawn. Boreal is a Latin word meaning *north*.

The second figure on this pole is a drowned man who has become a land otter. He holds on to logs to use as a canoe and live mink for paddles. Anyone who speaks to a land otter, or on whom it breathes, becomes one, too.

The devilfish at the bottom was carved to suggest a boulder-strewn, cave-dotted beach.

Use faster film; say 400, with a 25-40 second exposure. Increase or decrease exposure time in 30% increments.

Day 9:

Dog Salmon House in Tuxekan, like the rest of the houses in the village, has totally collapsed.

Some insist they can hear the Aurora—a swish or crackle similar to static on the radio. But others suggest such sound may actually be produced inside the head as a sort of phantom limb or tinnitus.

Fuji Supra 800 and Provia 400F.

Day 10:

Ravens make an astonishing variety of noises, from raucous squawks to hollow, warbling whistles. On winter days they have been seen warming themselves at the streetlamps, turning the lights on by covering the light-sensors with their wings to simulate darkness.

An easy way to test whether one can hear the Aurora Borealis would be to close your eyes during one and see if the sound goes away.

At the Garage Sale

On Friday, rain and a man from Padua. "Poets look at the world and compress it beautifully for us," he says.

We can't recall ever seeing it rain so much.

Later, two Canadian geese honk overhead and Wayne stands up and honks back at them. They turn and circle back to get a better look. He does this again to another pair. Wayne and the birds of the air.

Saturday, an osprey flies over, holding a bullhead in its talons. We look down at our wares.

During a lull, the man with the cashbox rocks and rocks on the edge of his chair, as if on water, as if in wind.

On a table, an array of Berlitz handbooks with phrases useful to the traveler:

> *Aardappelsoep*: Potato soup
> *Kan jeg fa et bord ved unduet*: May I have a table by the window?
> *Machen Sie bitte dies Rechnung fertig*: Please prepare my bill.

A fellow asks, "Have any books on human consciousness?"

We look up for a bird.

They had a hard time breathing and sleeping in the dusty city. Mopeds, smokers, diesels and tiny cars, their occupants shouting, waving and honking—all combined with the heat, the aging buildings, the wooden shutters to make everything penetrable and gritty and clouded up. Dust covered dust.

Sensing their fatigue, their friend took them on weekends to the hills, to the tall pines and hydrangea-rimmed gardens, the olive trees and green open spaces separating the villas. There they were soothed by the shiny dark wood floors of their hotel, the white starched linens and tall, loose curtains that made them feel they were in an elegant hospital. Inhaling deeply, they flopped onto the low beds and stretched their arms. *Ah, Italia!* they breathed, embracing the privileged mountains of patronage.

*

In the morning they dressed and joined their host for breakfast downstairs. They chose thick dark coffee, hard-crusted bread with smooth pats of butter, golden cheeses, chilled juice and chunks of colorful fruit and brilliant eggs with tissue-thin slices of ham. They ate and talked of the fine beds and afterward strolled in the gardens and wore their jackets draped on their shoulders as they had seen locals do and clasped their hands behind their backs as if they, too, were Continentals.

Soon they were driven back to the old city to continue their lectures and cough themselves to sleep. In their travelers' letters home, they described the smallest details of the hotel, the clouds, the enormous blue flowers, the spires of dark trees, the moments of blissful forgetfulness; though their friends all along had imagined them there, and only there—rested, jackets on their shoulders, at ease in the quiet groves, the hills, the airy land.

Vedute di Roma *(Views of Rome)*

Piranesi, drunk on his dreams of antiquity, was not surprised, coming home from a late night out in 1777, by the apparent movement of the front steps onto another plane. The dramatic change in the pattern of interlocked stone and timber—he had seen it before. The chiaroscuro, forceful and tightened … It was a form of greeting, intimate and private, between the man and his house, an homage to the elaborate designs he had seen for the apse of the Lateran Basilica.

As he approached, the steps separated themselves still more from the door and walk, shifting and floating, now connecting to each other by arch, now disconnecting by lapse. "Yes!" he said companionably, *"Carceri d'invenzione,"* the imaginary prisons. He recalled fondly the canal accesses to the church of the Knights of Malta on the Aventine, Santa Maria del Priorato, the impressive ceremonial piazza enclosed by obelisks and architectural trophies.

In the dark and cold he improvised in his mind a complicated assortment of winches, pulleys and slings to help him gain entrance to his house. By practical application of his hands and knees he progressed and was soon heard declaiming in the doorway, "I believe that if I were commissioned to design a new universe, I would be mad enough to undertake it."

On the day of his death he continued at work amid his drawings and copperplates. "Repose," he said, "is unworthy of a citizen of Rome."

The Statuary Garden

The Statuary Garden

I meant to write more about something else but was distracted by the de Chirico print, *L'Angoisse du depart*, a thing so confident of its place it could have chosen it in advance. I don't know why it feels like that, but that's what I felt and, principally, it made me remember the bulbs and what I had done to them. Asleep, dead, alive—who was I to say they had to be anything?

In a few days I had enacted one violence after another, now burying gladiolus, now wringing tea from bags I had exposed to light then scalded. Though the anguished leave, they seldom go intact.

De Chirico did not paint the box in the foreground of the painting; he painted the shadow on it, its impending absence, the explanatory puff in the distance, the voice it gives voice to. And the Dresdner monkey, the porcelain violinist in the Harry Lane print next to it, the tailed musician flanked by roses— Harry did paint that, but he did not paint the surprise of the petals, the reflection of framing glass on the green vase, the sigh from the drape, seductive as silk, as it falls across the table. I don't know how all those things even got there. It is not my fault—nor mine, the perturbations of light.

*

Part of me, my arm, my hand, descended into that unseen area below the desk—the place, as under a small shrub that does not need my thinking about—and began to fumble around in the dark of the floor for a pen that had rolled off the tabletop. The longer my hand was away from me, so to speak, out of sight and, it seemed, "at large," the more vulnerable I felt— part of me launched into any sort of possibility. I mean, who knows? My hand was by now almost a being of its own going resolvedly forth (though what it understood of true search I don't know.) In alarm, I bent down a bit more and leaned in so I could see it again—see if I still recognized it, if it would come when I called—and as I did so, for the briefest of moments, I thought I saw another hand approaching from the opposite direction, feeling toward mine as if to seek it out.

Well, I do not believe in mirrors and the evening was getting on and on, so I stood up and let the whole matter go.

*

I decided I wanted to build something near the lucifers—take out the rhododendron, erect a trellis or pergola or gazebo—to stake out change quickly while the beast next door, asleep and digesting, forgets a while to run at the fence, slam into it, barrel into it again and again, bending and cracking it until he can one day burst through, tearing his face, his fur, his feet with splinters and nails and causing God knows what.

*

She was there in the shade garden on the north side when I moved in: "Sophia," a cement statue that is also a circulating stone fountain, prominent among the hostas and Japanese maples, though obscured from the deck, the koi pond, the lindens, the round herb garden. Her head-mounted vessel is tipped, letting water spill relentlessly down her front and back, as if to baptize her to the point of disappearance. Standing and watching for just a few moments makes me tired, so I usually sit on the bench.

I can see no inscriptions other than her name so I cannot tell who made her or if she is Italian or Greek—she who splashes elegance so casually, as if it does not cost. As circular as yearning, like a ghost that cannot kiss, beauty poured to pour again—what good could come of this. She looks at me deliberately, like the moon.

The rest of the garden is sparsely planted, not overgrown, not anything for H. Rousseau—no red sun, no jaguar on the man or on the man's shadow (whichever it is that flees)—yet something dies in it just the same, year after year.

*

Beyond my fence, with its close-fitting boards, I believe there are trees in fine rich soil covering old lava sheets and, among the trees, luxuriant bunch grass.

Sometimes, walking back to the house, when I am halfway up the steps to the deck, I pause and hear the earth make its smallest movements.

*

My garden has a continental climate. Because of its steady march away from maritime influences, it is its own small region of mild relief ringed by larger classical forms: the orators, maidens and mythical beasts that I and others have installed. Beside the lilac, I place a sphere that hosts four equidistant bees.

I have identified this soil (loess), rocks, plains, hillocks, crests, ridges, hills, ranges and peaks—all of which, though I know nothing of fractals, repeat the facts of nature just as, by alchemical lettering, draftsmen making images bring objects into being.

In the mail, a packet of postcards: *La Porte Saint-Denis*, *The Pyramid of Cestius*, *The Teatro Anatomico of Padua*.

*

One night I turned the upstairs thermostat too low and woke up shuddering. In the shower, to warm up, I turned the water too high and reddened my shoulder. The spot, what I could see of it, looked like Corsica. Looking out the window I saw

robins tearing worms from the ground I had disturbed for the
bulbs.

*

My collections have grown to include a segment of columnar
basalt shaped like a birdbath, a cup with a map of the Inside
Passage, a brass counterweight marked "1000 grm." The row
of evergreens I planted in autumn clearly aspires, but may
never become tall and one tree is turning brown. I frame my
pictures and hang every one and save interesting things in
interesting boxes—creating a tidiness the way a nesting bird
uses twigs.

I worry that if I see a thing I like but don't buy it, I may never
encounter it again—a vexation common among the religious
and a boon to commerce—and so am always acting on what I
see, though closing my eyes tight at an overhang of rock.

*

Desire is the most unaccommodating sense. I often speak
about the pond in small texts; how snails sweep it clean every
day. I do not speak about the island.

One day, under water, all the pond animals died, all at once, I
don't know why, their skeletons and shells weaving together a
sort of reef.

85

*

A fellow came to paint the wood segments of the arbor rising
above the concrete slab just outside the family room slider—
that and a small bench. He did a great job and I thanked him
and admired his work, though I felt, I don't know why, I was
in another place altogether.

*

Sunday, the traditional morning of regret, I woke in worry in
the dark, my imagination awash with images of animals
scrabbling, branches breaking, beaks tearing the tendons that
hold things up, of fish tossed strangling onto stone. Anything
can happen in a place that has shown you its scars.

I am no naïf, I know that things disappear, vessels break and
founder, fingerprints go unidentified; a car does, machines do,
people and dogs do, doggedly, the most unimaginable things.
An unrelenting stratum of trouble rises to do its disruptive
best—though I like to presume that my familiars still wait for
me, unmolested, by the stairs.

I shook myself in alarm, threw on my clothes, snapped back
the shades, turned on the lights, washed the dishes, vacuumed
the carpets, straightened the pictures and adjusted the chairs
into smaller and tidier conversation groups.

Then I buckled up my high mud boots, put on my woolly coat with the two rows of buttons, pulled on my aviator's hat with the fur earflaps and strode stolidly toward the door.

I opened wide the slider to the backyard. My eyes took in everything and threatened to keep looking.

*

I believe that in their hearts even the smallest animals sense what they are.

My feet cramp. I seldom go out. Each sunny day hurts my eyes. My fingers tighten in the cold and turn white. At night my heart weighs itself against its better deeds and is not light.

Often I have appointments so plain I cannot even think what they are for.

*

Maybe, the Jesuits say, *Heaven is an instant, that white light.* In an Ignation spirit, I try sleeping on the opposite side of the bed. As if study were an end in itself.

And, among the withering rock face of a gorge, I examine whether some thoughts might add to us in ways that do not move us forward, whether we may be diminished instead;

whether we know what forward is, whether thought is not sometimes a thing.

*

In the photograph four people are holding up an oil painting. I don't know who painted the painting—perhaps it is a gift, a memory, a burden. Each holds a corner, steadying it for the camera. Sun cuts their faces in half. The oil looks sticky. It must have been hot weather that day and—nothing resolves in humid climes. The four seem to want to draw my attention to the painting and so I look.

If one were to diagram this painting, there would be lines, labels, indices, values, tones and elevations, but only one color plus black.

Above the presumed hill is a green Aurora Borealis that touches the green trees in a thrilling way and intermingles with their tops. The sense of where the sky lifts up or touches down is vague; and maybe, after all, this is instead a portrait of a green forest fire blazing up through the top of the picture and out by the edges and sure to singe those holders if they are not careful.

One of the people holding it has gout, one is a neighbor standing at a kind of attention and one has an earnest but failing heart. The woman at the right seems to be tired of holding up her end of the painting, perhaps worrying that she will die alone with it.

*

"No, no, no," the landscaper said. "The *fritillaria* go everywhere, not just the beds … for naturalizing." In that case, I despaired. Even more violence would be coming.

I slipped off my garden shoes. Obviously, I would have to think about things in a different way. I made coffee, slipped Sibelius into the CD player, and settled into a soft chair where the long rays of the sun warmed my shoulders through the window, encouraging them to stay.

*

The maintenance workers were finished and long gone when I noticed from the dining room window, which faces the pergola, that someone had picked up the small stone pelican from the gladiola bed and placed it between the arms of one of the stone sphinxes on the deck. I had lost track of the pelican, and now it had become a detail from Merson's *Rest on the Flight into Egypt*, a painting in which some of the Holy Family sleeps, apparently in the arms of a sphinx, but mostly in a strange light. Someone did not want the bird to get lost. The darker pages of scripture are one thing, haven and wing another, so I resisted going outside even to look closely and left everything as it was.

*

I don't know how I got to be so lucky. I can walk to most places from my home though it requires crossing traffic to do so. As cars around here do not normally slow even for their own kind, attention is called for, as is bright clothing and, if possible, more than average height. I am lucky to be so tall.

I had stopped at a bus kiosk to rest on the bench and managed to hum five or six parts of the *Goldberg Variations* before feeling I had better move on in case a bus should approach and see me and misinterpret everything.

The building next on my left going north was the co-op where prescription renewals awaited me for anti-allergens and acid blockers. I approached the two big out-swinging doors, anticipating the visual happiness of the rock wall sculpture inside, water softly running down the face of it, and the hall bearing two large prints of Italian villas—the lavenders, olives and pines! As I started to reach for the handle the door suddenly swung out toward me from within. I pulled back quickly, saving my fingers. Luck was everywhere with me that day.

Farther along the street, I noted that the hardware store had a sale on LED string icicles. Two would do for the arbor. Lately, evenings have been coming on too early, disappointing me when I still wanted light. I went in, switching in my mind from Glenn Gould to the orchestral version of the *Variations*— the popular arrangement despised by the *cognoscenti*.

At the deli, as the clerk made a sandwich for me, I saw a dishcloth come very close to touching my slice of bread. When my lunch was served, I peeled off the crust; though this exposed the interior and made containment less certain.

At that point I'd spent all the money I had on me, so I went home to bury myself in a book. A car honked at me as I cleared the road.

*

I don't know if Darwin discusses it, but sometimes breathing is hard and at any time anything can be futile. If he did say something about this, I don't know where to find it.

*

I drove out to buy a calendar but instead bought an urn, a lavish large pot with angelic creatures clinging to its top. With its rust and supporting square base it made me think of the urns of Versailles. I have no idea what perfection is or if it is affected by a deep rent down an angel's back, a gap in my mind as deep as the Mid-Atlantic Rift where it surfaces in Iceland. This gash had claimed one wing. The two contemplatives stood on lions' heads and gripped the rim, staring steadily into emptiness.

It is a habit of humans and nature to adapt. I thought I might sit on the bench and consider how these sprites manage but began to worry that if I looked too long, they might sense it and look up. So, I arose and went inside.

*

Often when gardening, I think of other places, places not even nearby, like Shorey's bookstore, the Roosevelt Café, or even Magnolia Hi-Fi where motivated young staff in suits used to show me the high-end equipment that makes sound larger and sharper and imparts a fineness that seems to come from an altogether new way of listening. Sometimes I just have to sit and let everything come at me from all sides.

*

It is tiring to tire so easily and I already had that morning as I approached the strip mall, so I was not particularly aware of my surroundings (though having been warned to be.) Suddenly two kids on skateboards roared up from behind and sped around me like twin trains, setting me spinning.

Well, I was unprepared for the blow. It knocked me off right my feet. I shouted after them, compiling pain from its furthest reaches and pumping it into a fist—a coiled peony wilting on the walk.

I believe in expectations as well as embarrassment so without looking around I got up in a wooden way and leaned my back against a light post for support. My hands, as they steadied me

92

against the metal, sensed its diameter grow narrower, as a tree might, the higher it rose from the ground. Planted much deeper than the four inches marked on a trowel for bulbs, the post had no sense or discomfort, no need to struggle, no surprise. It didn't need to bloom or please me in any way. I was humbled. *Bless the bulbs, the grass, the trees and all 'spiring things, in the name of this post*, I thought. I heard the words as if they were already in the air and for a moment did not know where I was.

Weeping Buddha

One story about Weeping Buddha is that he cries for the troubles of the world, thereby absorbing the common grief. The world is profoundly sad, and someone must always feel its sorrows so the rest of us can be joyful.

Some refer to his meditative posture—a rolled-up version of sitting such as that adopted by the hedgehog when startled—as a way to open and activate the third eye. It is also said, but not in a convincing way, that this pose is for the benefit of apprentice carvers who must first learn the form of the body before practicing the face, the way students of human dissection are required to work on the hands, feet and torso of the cadaver rather than confront, too soon, too nakedly, the gateway to the human: the muscles of facial expression.

An alternate story goes this way: Two warriors confront each other in numerous battles, each time wearing masks. After many such encounters in which neither saw the other's face, the older warrior kills the younger. Upon removing the mask of the vanquished, he discovers his lost son. He folds forward in sorrow.

If you touch Weeping Buddha, your sadness is supposed to pass into him.

In modern places like Germany, along the Weeping Willow Allee, one may encounter a Japanese-style fence and gate and, behind it, the Buddha resting between peony beds and other specialty plants.

Flags of battle in the ancient time of contest were carried on poles that were nearly as tall as the horses. The unbroken field, the looming violence, the crackling of leather and sinew all combined to create great winds that snapped and tore at the banners, pulling the standard bearers violently aside if they were not using all their strength to hold on. The eyes of their horses were huge and white. Without a battle, the rending of flags and the fright of the mounts alone might have decided something.

The reverse figure is Hotei or Laughing Buddha, whose stomach may be rubbed for good luck. Luck is not the opposite of sadness but similar to it, as death is to swamp weeds for a mallard.

*

I name all my cats Salo, after Kurt Vonnegut's emissary from beings on the planet Tralfamador who live all the times of their lives simultaneously—past, future, and an elaborately wide and punctuated present.

*

On the first night of the class in Modern American Poetry, the professor asks his graduate students to stand and read from their work to show the freshmen how it is to be done. Rather than write like a graduate student, I take up the Course Catalog again, browsing the courses of study, this time circling *Anthropology*—a discipline with many practical applications.

In class we learn:
… that the data of culture and social life are susceptible to exact scientific treatment
… that early scholars believed a "vital force" resided in enzymes, all the while discounting the primitive belief in the magical nature of tools
… that a number of arguments seems to prove the soul is eternal and indestructible and has existed for all eternity
… that the *palmaris longis*, a muscle in the middle of the human wrist, is sometimes fully developed and sometimes not even present
… that Livingstone's bearers said, at their first-ever glimpse of the sea: "We marched along with our father, believing that what the elders had always told us was true, that the world had no end; but all at once, the world said to us, *I am finished: there is no more of me.*"
… that captains of the Alaskan halibut fleets create their own language to keep the hot fishing spots secret.

I nail a four-inch halibut jig above my desk next to the knife of a kind made for at least one thousand years in Finland, a knife with the right reach for sticking. Depicting the head of a horse on its carved handle, mine hangs in a hand-tooled leather sheath with curved metal tip.

I can't believe my good fortune, in only the third quarter of school, to chance upon an auction not just of older horsehead knives, but of two other styles so far unknown to me: *Hirvikoirapuukko*, the wolf head, *Ajokoirapuukko*, the hound.

The miniature set of dominoes that no one else bid for, I set out on a small table. Beginning with one piece and adding more, one at a time, end-to-end, tilting each new piece toward the left, tight against the others, the complete set begins to illustrate the outward spiral of an ammonite.

I can hardly wait for my second year of study.

Next to the bust of Neanderthal in the living room I make an artful arrangement of miniature ceramic houses and hang, in the dining room, the 1940's print of a wolf on a snowy hill overlooking a sleeping town—tracks behind, village ahead, its own hot animal breath making a cloud, lights out below, horses safely stabled.

"Things can disappear," I tell Salo, recounting a lesson, "when you stop looking at them."

*

Across from my house, the promenade dividing the pavement of Ravenna Boulevard is green with grass and trees but also with unusual expanse, the designer perhaps bewildered by a concurrent rise and bend going forward and thinking this meant to add space. The old trees are deciduous, their leaves early on the route to being something else as, on that morning, from my window, what I see before me is not a boulevard but a glade.

Then, as so often, there is a solitary man walking the promenade. I name him Edouard, for the Merwin poem published in the New Yorker on my birthday—*Edouard shall we have gone when the leaves come out*—but no, it is the Dalai Lama, far from home, wakeful before studies. The street is still asleep. The grass is wide here, wider uphill. I am behind a glass and on my way to becoming mute. Gifts are uncertain and the soul a small bell.

*

Where I moved to, where I am living now, is a place unlike any I have lived in before or would choose if I had a choice among all—an opportunity that eludes me. It is warm and pleasant and though not particularly thrilling, my heart seems to work at this elevation as well as at any other, a condition which is the pride and pity of hearts everywhere.

Still, my streak of nostalgia is as wide as Ravenna Boulevard.

*

Strolling out from under the lace-leaf maples onto the fields of a local estate—yellow jackets investigating my hair, air pausing to deliberate its next move, quails clucking at magpies dragging their long tails over mowed-down wheat—in such moments there may bloom a feeling of patience and abundance as from the recollection of fine art. And the deer may be there, in watchful standing.

All this may be found in the literature of the world.

The afternoon gathers like a caterpillar. I pull a thistle from the lawn and tell the deer my name. The sun in sequent rings moves to another place. So do the deer. A bee picks out something it likes. A day goes by.

*

All my cats seem also to have one name for me, though which it is among the rich variety of sounds they make I cannot tell.

*

The whistle of the Burlington Northern slips through the window as the train snakes north and east along the water. Farther on, the train will set aim for Chicago, sounding its horn at intersections all across Montana. Its passengers are jounced in their berths, wrapped in their own lonely sounds, dreaming from a distance of pinpoint arrivals.

As the train wanders away, its lingering vibrations travel out from the wheels, down through iron spikes grounding the rails, into the trucked-in rock of the rail bed. From there they radiate through glacial till until reaching the foundations of my house which, though confident and sturdy, shudders slightly. Inside, I sleep the sleep of the communicant.

*

I have candies in my pocket. I am older than I was. I have a favorite cup, have written a sentence and changed it. I am reading *Transformations of St. Ekaterina of Alexandria*, a book which seems to have nothing to do with me, and I will soon move on to *Thérèse* by Francois Mauriac, though that has little to do with me either.

*

A friend writes: *Do you remember that closed-up house in Des Moines—empty and overgrown—we had to fight our way to the front window—a small house—and inside, well, we couldn't see all the way in, but we could make out that huge desk—all cubby-holes and small drawers—piled high with papers? I wondered then as I do now how anyone could have left it.*

It is hard exactly to remember loss. Sometimes the injured animal does not, after all, turn toward you or open its eyes. Or in the absolute of your silent cold dream when ground dissolves and you start to float away, suddenly a noise or light announces the renewal of the world—but sloppily, unsatisfactorily, and without key elements. Sometimes a sink-hole opens in your chest or there is a slippage of geologic plates, or lines unravel from cleats, or pieces of something clink and echo all the way down a cistern that is only half-full. Sometimes you hear the hammering of wind and rain and, sometimes, there is simply absence and more and more of it.

*

At the free symphony concert that begins all musical seasons, before the conductor steps on stage, I hear a kind of rustling and look up to see a small group of nuns entering the aisle opposite, their habits sweeping side to side like long, black hair. As they turn to sit, I can see that only the surface fabric is black. It covers very dark blue and, of course, white. One does not wish to think too much about it. They settle, dark magmas of cloth overflowing the armrests.

I hardly ever see a nun inside a public building. Most often one encounters them in pairs on sidewalks where they appear to be moved as much by wind as by themselves, their eyes down, hands hidden—one of the forms that constancy pins its hopes on.

As the nuns gather their rivers of cloth around them for sitting, a wooden bead clacks on metal—once, then once again— discreet as the beads of a nun should be.

I remember that I too am wearing a uniform and in a conversational gesture reach up to feel the chain at my neck from which hangs a gold cap that holds, as surely as once did the gums, the incisor of a chimpanzee.

*

When the cat goes out one night and fails to return, he takes all the good ideas with him.

I go to the door to listen for him. The world before me suddenly enlarges and at the same time funnels down close. *Everywhere* is there at once. I hear a loggerhead shrike knife through the shrubby steppes in the shadows of Cedar Breaks in Utah. Holding onto the cold door handle, I think of the anchor cable sticking up from the humus of Arbor Lake in Seattle, before it trails down into the peaty murk. A "dead man," they'd called it, the drowning end of mortal coil. Farther out I see people wearing rags and masks as they climb the crisscross legs of towering rigs—the masts of the oil fields of the Caucasus feeding the appetites of the great engines.

Nearer to me, over the rooftop chimneys, the silhouettes of trees seem to be waving for help.

The Buddha curls forward, his palms gently coaxing his head closer to his heart.

At 3rd and Division, at the light, two full lanes of cars have quietly appeared alongside on my right, kept from my lane by a fence of concrete wedges.

At the signal change, I creep forward in a low gear. The two lanes to the left come along with me; the isolated fourth on that side is held back. It seems the entire world wants to enter the city. Gradually, the far-left lane disappears, and those that were on the right, released when I wasn't watching, now join in behind, scattering across lanes like fire ants. Spokane: A city to be reckoned with.

I am here to complete my studies.

On my way through the cities and universities of the world, I have driven a number of cars, each of them red. In the totemic arrangements of the Pacific Northwest red is the color of life, black, the spirit world. For example, Uncle Red died in Skagit County in a black Chevrolet sedan.

In the complex circuits of Haida and Kwakiutl mythology, in the earliest days, all forms (raven, sun, man, bear, etc.) were interchangeable. I am not the one to say what holds true, here in my Rover TC 3500 on the Columbia Plateau—which sits on ancient lava flows as sublimely as a monkey tops a tree; as reliably as the pelvis balances on its femurs; as purposefully as a gargoyle holds on to the wall and spews water.

The rear-drive engine propels me gondola-style. Floating birds and ruffling animals at the roadside provide a lyricism found in the rococo. Renewing rivers and recurrent themes of epiphany offer variety. Experience always must be delicately balanced, endearing yet respectful, only barely pious, and there may be the insertion of romantic, pastoral characters that later prove popular with landscape painters.

*

The familiar comprises the most foreign of influences. After all, a knight who, as a child, had been sold by his mother into slavery, ultimately regained his patrimony by marrying the King of Armenia's daughter.

And though one was not permitted to bear arms inside the old Mercato Nuovo of Florence, neither could one be arrested inside it for debt.

On the other hand, I am wary of slipping my feet into high-top slippers for fear of what may be already inside.

And one day on Puget Sound, an even layer of clouds (such as composed my frequent companions) appeared to be marching down the sky before and at the same rate as the sun. A picture of the event resides in the glove box. Yet, the reflected line of sunlight that crosses the surface of the water—a straight line coming right at me—is not broken by that cloudy gap.

All of this, of course, is correct in science and history; not so much in the registering of it. There are whole areas of thought to be worked out and some items—snack foods and hair products, for instance—may not be available where one ends up. I note the exact time of departure. Someone always leaves the door of the world open; one must be careful not to fall out of it.

*

I drive into the parking lot of the School of Architecture and Fine Design. (At home, the quail line up on the fence and wonder if it is safe to drop down into the yard.)

I diagram the images as described. In this construction, as in all things, the old core remains though there have been alterations everywhere.

Another building is a fine specimen of the flamboyant, having most of its beauties of style and few of its faults. It has been a long time since coffee, and I have some trouble depicting the main hall with stone recesses reserved for the sick who are laid there to be cured during the night by saints.

In this example, carved images of trees, a shepherd and quizzical sheep appear to have been adapted from Catiglione's version of The Flight, making me want to declaim Matthew Arnold as I exit: *The sea is calm tonight, The tide is full, the moon lies fair Upon the Straits....*

*

The tail of the raven in flight is wedge-shaped, distinguishing it from the fan shape of the crow. A fantail is the stern overhang of a ship. One may name the ship *Concordia.*

Sometimes my mind is so full I must dismount and proceed on foot, supported by the angels.

*

A small section of the Natatorium was popularly called *Pentimento* after Pentti Karkiainen, cook's apprentice and lute player. Initially considered an oddity, he came to be regarded affectionately for his afternoon concerts in the garden. Resonance was heightened by his barely concealed sorrow for a life of misdeeds, the details of which were never fully revealed and, for all the listeners knew, may have been made up for effect—and anyway likely occurred in another country. The peculiar tuning of his instrument is still imitated.

*

I ease into the parking lot of the School of Agriculture. (Back in my house the cat paces and sleeps, paces and sleeps, prepared at any moment to be indifferent.)

Thus far we have emphasized the importance of favorable conditions. Soils are adaptable media, as are particular offices of the Archdiocese. Through interventions, elements taken from the ground are returned to it. That the earth eventually yields up vast storehouses is a fortune taken on faith.

An oil painting purchased at auction has handwriting on the back: *I can see all the dinosaurs from Uncle Jim's ranch.* Humus is life, everything else is mystery.

*

Snow had fallen intermittently on my drive up to and back from Mt. Spokane, but apparently was consistent and heavy at my home, the reverse of what I would expect. I believe in the present, that the shadows of clouds on the ground are as high and wide as the real things above—not the theory of the shaken globe, exactly, but like canvases with the backgrounds already carefully painted in—so disproportion startles me.

Snow is sitting in the branches of the flowering pear and golden chain trees and now peers at me, wondering who I am. Staying in the center of the porch, away from the long bolts of icicles on the eaves, I struggle up the steps, lifting my cold knees high like slow, old pumps.

Inside, things are as they had been. I change into fleece and make tea.

Weather modeling is practiced by meteorologists and amateurs all over the world, local readings taken from instruments placed at any sustainable place—or, just as frequently, by someone simply turning their head toward or away from the side being pelted by the elements.

*

The European Fish Ageing Network (EFAN) uses the otolith to age halibut, reading only those collected from the left or blind side. Halibut grow faster the farther north you go: a 40 lb fish off the coast of Washington is likely to be much older than one off Kodiak. I live in the South Hill area of Spokane and am aging fast.

*

We may now turn to the consideration of the Hominoidea in some detail. As night approaches, the gorilla builds a nest that it uses once then abandons. The lowland gorilla usually sleeps in trees, while mountain gorillas prefer the ground and occasionally a space under a rock ledge.

The human fear of standing under a ledge may be overcome by habitually seeking out a sunny place to stand.

Gorillas are slow moving on ground and may be easily overtaken/// *It happens again. Driving north on Lincoln, not only does the far-left lane completely disappear, but I am forced into a direction I do not want at all.*

*

I am told, and have read, that I was born at 4.35 A.M. in a room barricaded against the cold of November. I imagine there was music, swelling out toward me like nourishment; all kinds of musical shapes in flow. Or maybe not music, but voices— voices of soft blended light circling my head like butterflies that must privately have thought me a strange, sad plant.

*

A crust under force forms corrugations, prominences, hollows. Monuments of the desert valley leak calcium and are drilled by wind, creating empty arches as folds die out below. The bones of an aging neck turn to stone, a family to dust. One may buy silk to warm a fusing core, but only slightly slow the loss of heat which, sensing freedom on the outside, flies toward it.

*

I seek another place to live. In the sculpture of discard, above the architrave, the marble bride tightens. Accumulations are not easily pried away; nor is the small, granite bouquet. And that assumption that nature will preserve its own slower, sweeter shapes is often deleted in the edits.

*

Every tree, a nest—but for the sake of clarity we must return to the tuning of stringed instruments.

I like gavottes and tarantellas while preparing dinner but switch to something more cello for the meal.

All systems undergo change over time. It is best, generally, to hold on to something—like the watercolors of Whidbey Island, the Olympic Peninsula, the California coast, or the Inuit stone carving of a breaching whale. Or agates. Agates are good.

Every nest, a tree.

*

So far we have discussed various systems for approaching the relentless turn of the seasons.

Machines that increase efficiency—the gang plow, section harrow, thresher, etc.—power the muscles of the day, but nothing, for those wakeful in the discomfiting night, speeds the hands of a clock along in darkness from one safe number to the next.

*

By now Lytton Strachey has complained in a letter to Virginia Woolf that there are times when he seems to see life steadily and see it whole but those are only moments and, as a rule, he can make nothing out.

Virginia has answered, "Next time, I mean to stick closer to facts."

*

Ravens hover in place like kestrels, soar like hawks. Each day I drive with Matthew Arnold *Out of the light and mutely.*

*

More secretive than anyone, JMW Turner had a strong instinct for painting as performance and was generally one of the first to arrive at the Royal Academy, coming down before breakfast and continuing his labor for as long as daylight lasted.

Robert Leslie remarked: "Besides red lead, he had a blue which … tempered with crimson or scarlet … he worked over his near waters in the darker lanes."

When Augustus Wall Callcott was asked what Turner was doing, he said: "I should be sorry to be the man to ask him."

*

Spokane moves mostly north and south, the river taking the east-west burden. Sometimes I jump right up for no reason at all to get in the car and drive around—a quadrupedal habit in the biped. I end up where predicted, even if lanes taking me there are capricious. And when I get there someone always feels compelled to speak.

I prefer the Palouse, the vast quilt of farms and hollows that rolls out from the edge of town to cover the south and east. Roads meander across the old flood plains from the Ice Age by means of weaves, dips and mounds, now turning for barns and pieces of towns, now for creeks and silos, now for a river and gorge with an enormous waterfall—each rise opening to spectacular beauty.

The colors of the earth (for there are few trees) mark the time of year—honey golds and greens, dull reds and whites, yellows, oranges, dark browns stiff with frost. It is possible that color is the beating heart there and one can be alone in it.

I have seen such paintings: a red skiff; a lifting tern; waves of dew on groundcover sparkling like an undulate sea.

Distance in the Palouse is both stark and soft. The reach of it goes farther and farther from the eye—nothing new in it but the wind. It could be that those old silt dunes believe they will outlast the soul.

When I stood in the rain forests of the Pacific Northwest, my wet reflection turned inward. Here, a part of me has wandered out of sight. I hope to retrieve it before the snow.

KATHRYN RANTALA is the author of *3 Letters & Julius* (2018) and *The Finnish Orchestra* (2013), and others. Her extensive assortment of journal credits includes *The Notre Dame Review, The Denver Quarterly, 3rd Bed, Cake Train, elimae, Alice Blue, New Orleans Review, Archipelago, Drunken Boat, The Oregon Review, Raven Chronicles, Diagram, Pear Noir!, Big Other*, and, in Paris, *Upstairs at Duroc*. She was nominated in 2022 for a second Pushcart Prize and has five poems included in the *Big Other Anthology 2022*. Her short story, "Metropolitana," received the LitPot Short Story Award, judged by Walter Cummins, and at one time she held the title for most lifetime nominations for the Rhysling Poetry award. A past reader for the William Stafford Poetry Award and the Washington Poets Association contest, she is a long-time resident of Edmonds, Washington, where she founded Ravenna Press and the journals *Snow Monkey* (with poet Christiel Cottrell) and *The Anemone Sidecar*.

9 781959 556718